**DO NOT REMOVE
CARDS FROM POCKET**

9/96

**ALLEN COUNTY PUBLIC LIBRARY
FORT WAYNE, INDIANA 46802**

You may return this book to any agency, branch,

or bookmobile of the Allen County Public Library.

DEMCO

The
Shopping Basket

John Burningham

CANDLEWICK PRESS
CAMBRIDGE, MASSACHUSETTS

Copyright © 1980 by John Burningham

Second U.S. edition 1996
First published by Jonathan Cape by whose permission
the present edition is published.

Library of Congress Cataloging-in-Publication Data is available.

ISBN 1-56402-688-4

10 9 8 7 6 5 4 3 2 1

Printed in Hong Kong

This book was typeset in Berkeley Old Style.
The pictures were done in pencil, ink, and watercolor.

Candlewick Press
2067 Massachusetts Avenue
Cambridge, Massachusetts 02140

"Run down to the store for me, will you, Steven, and buy six eggs, five bananas, four apples, three oranges for the baby, two doughnuts, and a bag of chips for your snack. And leave this note at Number 25."

So Steven set off for the store, carrying his basket. He passed Number 25,

the gap in the fence,

the full litter basket,

the men digging up the sidewalk,

and the house where the nasty dog lived,

and arrived at the store.

He bought the six eggs, five bananas, four apples, three oranges for the baby, two doughnuts, and a bag of chips for his snack. But when he came out of the store, there was a bear.

"I want those eggs," said the bear, "and if you don't give them to me, I will hug all the breath out of you."

"If I threw an egg up in the air," said Steven, "you are so slow I bet you couldn't even catch it."

"Me slow!" said the bear . . .

And Steven hurried on home carrying his basket. But when he got to the house where the nasty dog lived, there was a monkey.

"Give me those bananas," said the monkey, "or I'll pull your hair."

"If I threw a banana onto that doghouse, you're so noisy I bet you couldn't get it out without waking the dog."

"Me noisy!" said the monkey . . .

So Steven hurried on home carrying his basket. But when he got to where the men were digging up the sidewalk, there was a kangaroo.

"Give me those apples you have in your basket," said the kangaroo, "or I'll punch you."

"If I threw an apple over that tent, you're so clumsy I bet you couldn't even jump over and get it."

"Me clumsy!" said the kangaroo . . .

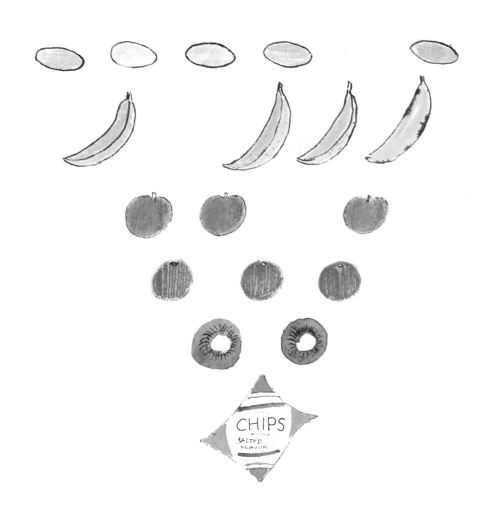

And Steven hurried on home carrying his basket. But when he got to the litter basket, there was a goat.

"Give me the oranges you have in your basket," said the goat, "or I'll butt you over the fence."

"If I put an orange in that litter basket, you're so stupid I bet you couldn't even get it out."

"Me stupid!" said the goat . . .

So Steven hurried on home carrying his basket. But when he got to the gap in the fence, there was a pig.

"Give me those doughnuts," said the pig,
"or I'll squash you against the fence."
  "If I put the doughnuts through that gap
in the fence, you're so fat I bet you
couldn't squeeze through and get them."
  "Me fat!" said the pig . . .

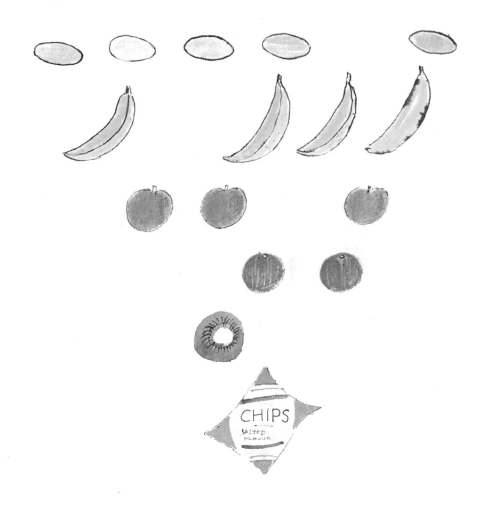

So Steven hurried on home carrying his basket. But when he got to Number 25, there was an elephant.

"Give me those chips," said the elephant,
"or I'll whack you with my trunk."
  "If I put these chips through that mail
slot, your trunk is so short I bet you couldn't
even reach them."
  "My trunk short!" said the elephant . . .

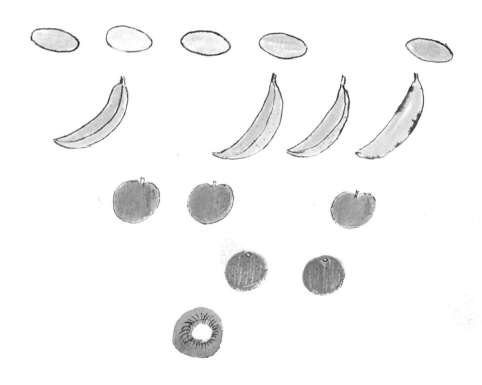

And Steven hurried on home carrying his basket. But when he got to his own house, there was his mother.

"Where on earth have you been, Steven? I only asked you to get six eggs, five bananas, four apples, three oranges, two doughnuts, and a bag of chips. How could it have taken so long?"